Bible Stories
from the Old Testament

Retold by Heather Amery
Illustrated by Norman Young
Designed by Maria Wheatley
Language consultant: Betty Root
Series editor: Jenny Tyler

Noah's Ark

This is Noah and his family.

Noah was a farmer who lived a long time ago.
He had a wife and three sons. Each son had a wife.

Noah was a good man.

He worked hard, growing food for his family.
Noah always did what God told him to do.

God talked to Noah.

He said, "The people are wicked. I'm going to flood the Earth and destroy them all, except you."

"Noah, you must build an ark."

"You must build it like this," said God. "Then you will save all the creatures in the world."

Noah started work.

His sons helped him. They marked out the shape
of the ark on the ground and cut down trees.

Noah and his sons worked hard.

They made a wooden frame. They put tar inside
and outside the ark to make it waterproof.

At last, the ark was ready.

Noah and his sons loaded it with lots of food for their family and food for all the creatures.

Then the creatures came.

There were two of every kind. Noah stared at them.
"I didn't know there were so many," he said.

They all went into the ark.

"God was right," said Noah. "The ark he told me to build is just big enough for all of us."

Then it started to rain.

It rained for forty days and nights. The ark floated away with them all safely inside.

The flood lasted for months.

Noah said to a raven, "Go and find some dry land."
The raven flew away but soon came back.

Later Noah sent off a dove.

It came back with a twig. Noah said, "The flood is over at last and everything is growing again."

Noah opened the door of the ark.

All his family and all the creatures rushed out.
The sun was shining and the land was dry.

14

"Spread out and have families."

"Live all over the Earth," God said to the creatures.
"Noah, your family must do this too."

God put a rainbow in the sky.

"That's my sign," said God. "I promise I'll never flood the whole Earth again." "Thank you," said Noah.

16

Joseph
and his
Amazing
Coat

This is Joseph with Jacob, his father.

Joseph had eleven brothers. Benjamin was the youngest. They lived in Canaan long ago.

Jacob loved Joseph best.

He gave Joseph a wonderful coat. Joseph's brothers were very jealous and hated him.

Joseph looked splendid in his coat.

One brother said, "Let's kill him." But another said, "No, let's sell him as a slave."

The brothers put blood on Joseph's coat.

They took it home. "Father," they said, "this is
Joseph's coat." Jacob thought Joseph was dead.

Joseph was taken to Egypt to be sold.

"I'll buy him," said Potiphar, captain of the King's guard. "He can run my house for me."

Potiphar's wife made trouble for Joseph.

"He's rude to me," she said. It was not true, but
Potiphar had Joseph put in prison.

The King had a strange dream.

He dreamed that seven fat cows came out of the Nile. Then seven very thin cows came out.

24

"What does it mean?" said the King.

The King's wise men and priests did not know. One said, "Joseph is good at telling what dreams mean."

"Bring Joseph here," said the King.

"Your dream means good harvests for seven years. Then seven bad years," said Joseph.

Joseph was put in charge of harvests.

During the seven good years, he stored lots of food away. Then the seven bad, hungry years came.

Jacob sent his sons to buy food.

Joseph saw them. "They are my brothers," he thought, "but they don't know who I am."

The brothers took the food home.

On the way, guards stopped them. In a sack they found a gold cup. Joseph had hidden it there.

The brothers were taken to Joseph.

"You may go home, but you must leave your
brother, Benjamin, here with me," said Joseph.

"Please keep us."

"Let Benjamin go home or it will break our father's heart," the brothers said.

Joseph saw his brothers had changed.

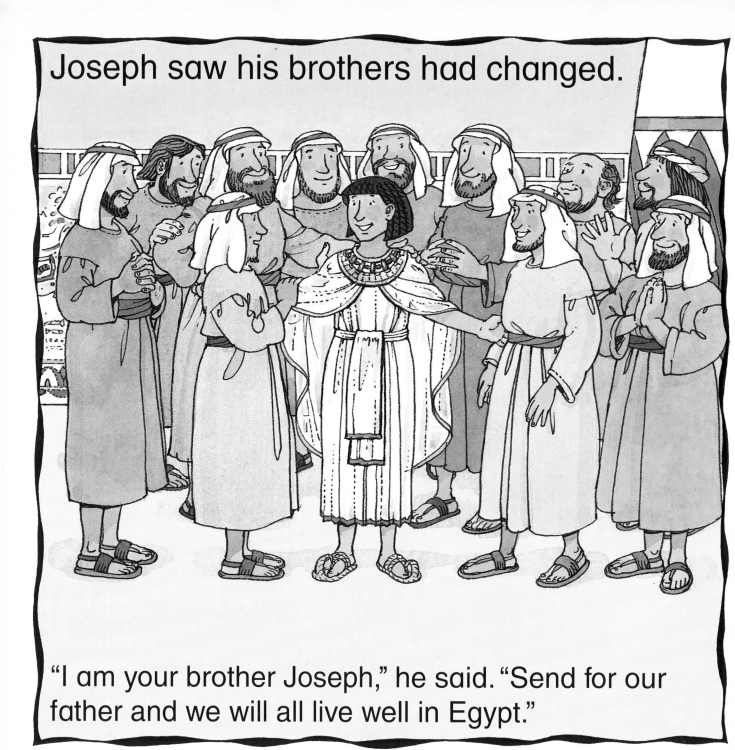

"I am your brother Joseph," he said. "Send for our father and we will all live well in Egypt."

Moses in the Bulrushes

This is baby Moses.

He is just three months old. He was born in Egypt a very long time ago.

Moses' parents were Hebrews.

The Egyptians made the Hebrews work very hard
building cities and temples.

This is the King of Egypt.

He was a cruel man. He was afraid the Hebrews would not obey the people of Egypt.

"The baby boys must die."

The King ordered his soldiers to find all the
Hebrew baby boys and kill them.

Moses' mother decided to hide her son.

"Please don't cry," she said. She was afraid the Egyptian soldiers would find him and kill him.

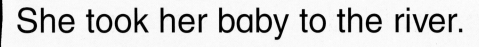

She took her baby to the river.

Moses' mother went to the Nile. She cut down lots of bulrushes and made them into a big basket.

She put Moses in the basket.

She kissed him and put the basket down on the water. The basket floated away.

40

Moses' sister was on the river bank.

She watched the basket. She followed it as it floated down the river.

Moses was asleep in the basket.

It floated past the Princess of Egypt. She was bathing in the water with her maids.

The Princess saw the basket.

"What's that?" she said. "Bring it here."
One of the maids picked up the basket.

The Princess looked at Moses.

Moses woke up and cried. "What a lovely baby," said the Princess. "He must be a Hebrew boy."

Moses' sister ran to the Princess.

"Do you want a Hebrew nurse for the baby?" she said. "Yes, bring one to me," said the Princess.

Moses' sister went to get her mother.

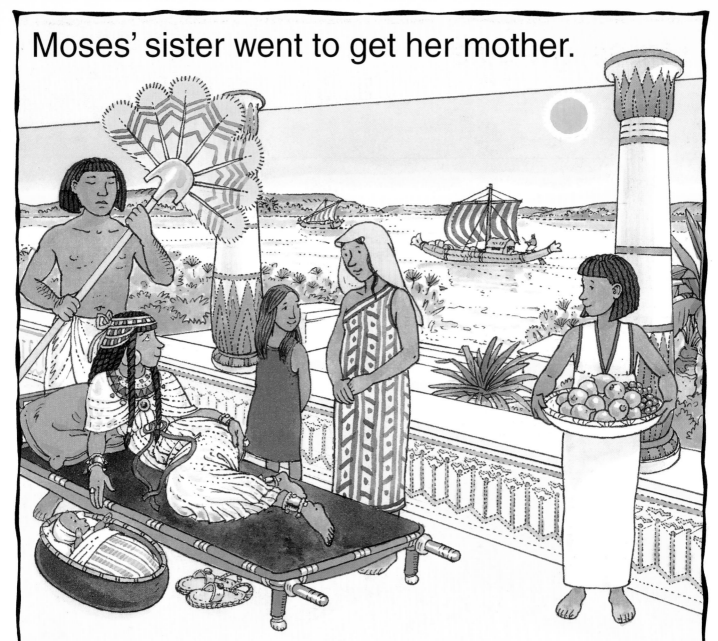

"Look after this baby," said the Princess. "I will pay
you well." Moses' mother took him home.

Moses was safe.

He grew up with his own family. When he was old enough, his mother took him back to the Princess.

47

"He's my son now," said the Princess.

Moses lived in the palace like an Egyptian prince.
But he never forgot he was a Hebrew.

This is David.

He lived a long time ago in Israel. He looked after his father's sheep out on the hills.

David was very brave.

He fought lions and bears which tried to kill the sheep. He thought God kept him safe.

He went to the army camp.

David's father asked him to take food to his three brothers. They were soldiers in King Saul's army.

The two armies watched
each other.

King Saul's army looked across the valley. They saw
their enemies, the Philistines, on the other side.

One soldier was a giant.

His name was Goliath. He was a huge and very strong man. He had a spear and a sword.

Every day he shouted a challenge.

"Send one man to fight me," he yelled. But King Saul's soldiers were too scared to go.

"I will fight him," said David.

"You are only a boy," said King Saul. "God has helped me to kill bears and lions," said David.

"You may go," said King Saul.

"But you must wear my fighting clothes." David put them on but they were much too big and heavy.

David took off the clothes.

He picked up five small stones for his sling. Then he walked across the valley to fight Goliath.

Goliath laughed at him.

"Come here, boy," he said, "and I will kill you."
David said, "God will help me to fight you."

David put a stone in his sling.

He swung it around his head, faster and faster.
He let it go and the little stone flew out.

The stone hit Goliath.

It hit the giant right in the middle of his forehead.
He fell down on the ground.

David ran up to Goliath.

The giant lay quite still. David saw that he was dead. The little stone had killed him.

King Saul's army cheered.

The Philistine soldiers were frightened and they ran away. King Saul's army chased them.

David had won.

All the people in Israel were delighted by his victory.
They danced and sang songs about David.

Daniel
and the
Lions

This is Daniel.

He lived a long time ago in Jerusalem. When he was young, the city was captured by an enemy army.

Daniel was taken to Babylon.

He lived with other boys. They had good food and went to school. Daniel prayed to God every day.

Daniel grew up very wise.

He lived at the King's palace. He was very good at telling people what their dreams meant.

He was made a ruler.

He was put in charge of two other rulers and many princes. They ruled the country for the King.

The two rulers hated Daniel.

They wanted to get rid of him. They tried to find something he had done wrong but Daniel was good.

The two rulers went to the King.

"King Darius," they said, "make a law that everyone must pray only to you or they must die."

Daniel heard about the law.

He would not obey it. He knelt by his window three times every day and prayed to God.

The two rulers watched him.

They hid among the trees. Then they went off to tell
the King about Daniel.

The King was very sad.

He liked and trusted Daniel. But he had made a
law and Daniel had broken it. Daniel must die.

Daniel was arrested.

He was put into a pit full of hungry lions. "May your God protect you," the King shouted to Daniel.

The King went to his palace.

He was so upset, he didn't want anything to eat and he couldn't sleep. He sent his servants away.

The King went to the lion pit.

It was very early the next morning. "Daniel, did your God save you?" he shouted down into the pit.

"I'm here, Oh King."

"God sent his angel to stop the lions from killing me," said Daniel. "God knows I've done no wrong."

The King was delighted.

He had Daniel set free. Then he told his guards to put the two rulers and the princes into the pit.

The King made a new law.

He ordered everyone in his kingdom to pray to
Daniel's God. God had saved Daniel from the lions.

This is Jonah.

He lived a very long time ago in a country called Israel. He was a good man who believed in God.

"Go to Nineveh," said God.

"The people there are very wicked. Tell them to be good and obey me."

Jonah didn't want to go.

"I'll go to Tarshish," he thought. "God won't be able to see me there." And he set off.

At the port he got on a ship.

Jonah paid his fare and the ship left for Tarshish.
But soon there was a terrible storm.

The sailors were terrified.

They prayed to their gods to save them but the storm got worse. Jonah slept through it all.

The captain woke Jonah.

"Ask your God to save us," he said. Jonah was trying to hide from God so he wouldn't pray.

"Throw me into the sea."

"That will save you," said Jonah. "I can't," said the captain. But some men grabbed Jonah.

They threw Jonah overboard.

Just at that moment, the storm stopped. The sailors thanked Jonah's God for saving them.

Jonah sank down into the sea.

"I am going to drown," thought Jonah. Suddenly a huge whale swam up and swallowed Jonah whole.

"God has saved me."

"I'm still alive," thought Jonah. "It's very dark and wet inside this whale."

Jonah lived in the whale for three days.

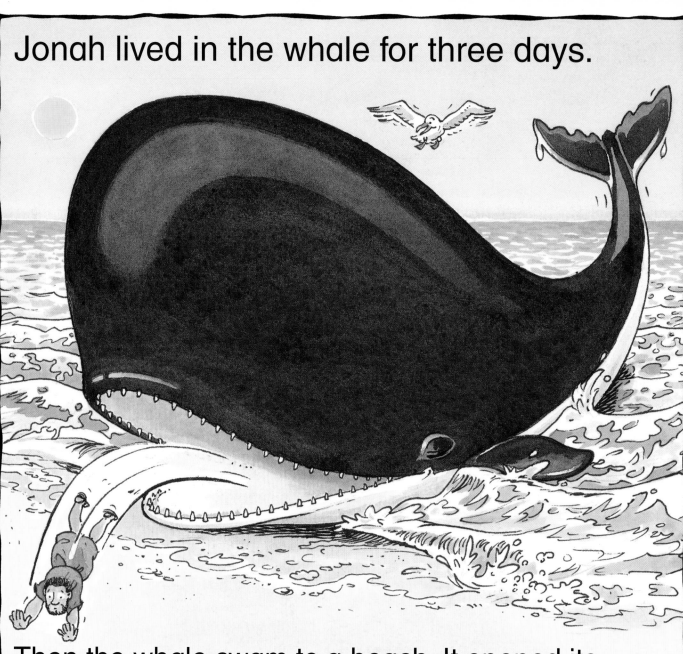

Then the whale swam to a beach. It opened its mouth and spat Jonah out onto dry land.

"Go to Nineveh," said God.

"All right, God. I'll go now," said Jonah and he walked all the way to the great city.

"You must stop being wicked," said Jonah.

"Or God will destroy your city." The King told the people that they must obey God.

Jonah sat outside the city.

He waited for it to be destroyed. But God saw that the people had changed and spared the city.

"I love all the people, Jonah."

"And I am everywhere," said God. "You can't run away from me." Jonah knew this was true.

First published in 1998 by Usborne Publishing Ltd, 83-85 Saffron Hill, London EC1N 8RT, England. Copyright © 1998, 1997, 1996 Usborne Publishing Ltd. The name Usborne and the device ☂ are Trade Marks of Usborne Publishing Ltd. All rights reserved. No part of this publication may be reproduced, stored in a retrieval system, or transmitted in any form or by any means, electronic, mechanical, photocopying, recording or otherwise, without prior permission of the publisher. UE First published in America in 1999. Printed in Belgium.